GOODNIGHT, WEST★TEXAS

Callie Fuqua

Illustrated by Richard Cowdrey

New York Times Bestselling Artist

BROWN BOOKS KIDS

Goodnight, West Texas

Brown Books Kids
Dallas / New York
www.BrownBooksKids.com
(972) 381-0009

A New Era in Publishing®

Publisher's Cataloging-In-Publication Data

Names: Fuqua, Callie, author. | Cowdrey, Richard, illustrator.
Title: Goodnight, West Texas / Callie Fuqua ; illustrated by Richard Cowdrey.
Other titles: Good night, West Texas
Description: Dallas ; New York : Brown Books Kids, [2024] | Audience: Juvenile. | Summary: There are so many lovely things about West Texas--how could we possibly say "goodnight" to them all? The sun is setting, and West Texas needs to go to bed--and so do we!--but first, let's say "Goodnight" to some of the places and things that make West Texas special.-- Publisher.
Identifiers: ISBN: 978-1-61254-693-3 (hardcover)
Subjects: LCSH: Texas, West--Description and travel--Juvenile literature. | Bedtime--Juvenile literature. | Country life--Texas, West--Juvenile literature. | CYAC: Texas, West--Description and travel. | Bedtime. | Country life--Texas, West. | BISAC: JUVENILE NONFICTION / Travel. | JUVENILE NONFICTION / Science & Nature / General. | JUVENILE NONFICTION / Lifestyles / Country Life.
Classification: LCC: F386.3 .F86 2024 | DDC: 976.49--dc23

This book has been officially leveled by using the F&P Text Level Gradient™ Leveling System.

ISBN 978-1-61254-693-3
LCCN 2024943622

Printed in China
10 9 8 7 6 5 4 3 2 1

For more information or to contact the author, please go to
www.CallieFuqua.com.

Dedication

For Lee, Henry, and Eloise—

my fifth- and seventh-generation West Texans.

Acknowledgments

Many thanks to the places, businesses, and organizations

mentioned in this book (and many, many more) that truly

make West Texas a wonderful place to live and visit.

It is time to take off our boots
and brush our wind-blown hair.

Goodnight, West Texas.
We are grateful for all you share.

Goodnight to the Concho River
flowing through San Angelo.

Goodnight, M.L. Leddy's.
For custom boots,
you must go.

Goodnight
to all the animals
at the Abilene Zoo.

Goodnight
to the giraffes
we love feeding
lettuce to.

Goodnight, Perini Ranch, "Best Little Steakhouse" in the West.
Goodnight, West Texas. It's time to get some rest.

Goodnight,
Sweetwater wind turbines
scattered through
fields of cotton.

Goodnight, Rattlesnake Roundup.
Your rattling tails won't be forgotten.

COMANCHE TRAIL PARK

Goodnight,
Comanche Trail Park,
the place where Big Spring
got its name.

Goodnight, Hotel Settles.
"Tallest Building in the West"
was your claim to fame.

Goodnight, Midland, booming oil town.
In your own way, you sure are pretty.

Goodnight, Odessa Meteor Crater,
a big, wide hole in the ground.

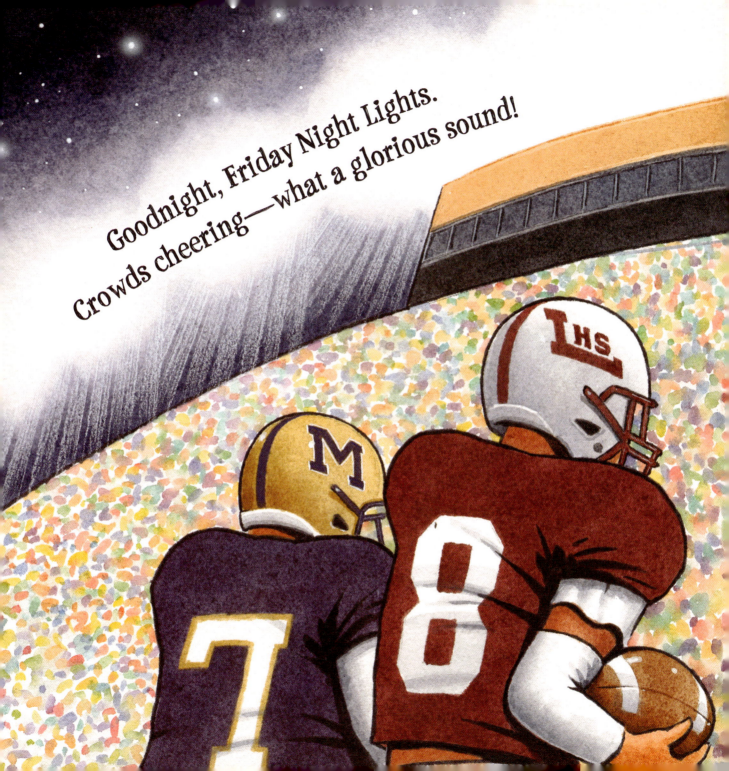

Goodnight, Friday Night Lights.
Crowds cheering—what a glorious sound!

Goodnight,
Monahans Sandhills,
where we love to sled down.

Goodnight,
West Texas people.
You are the friendliest around!

Goodnight, Pecos Rodeo,
the very first of its kind.

Goodnight, bull riders, ropers,
and more, who still go there to shine.

Goodnight,
Balmorhea State Park,
with swimming, camping,
and other fun play.

Goodnight,
dust devils and tumbleweeds,
blowing by on a windy day.

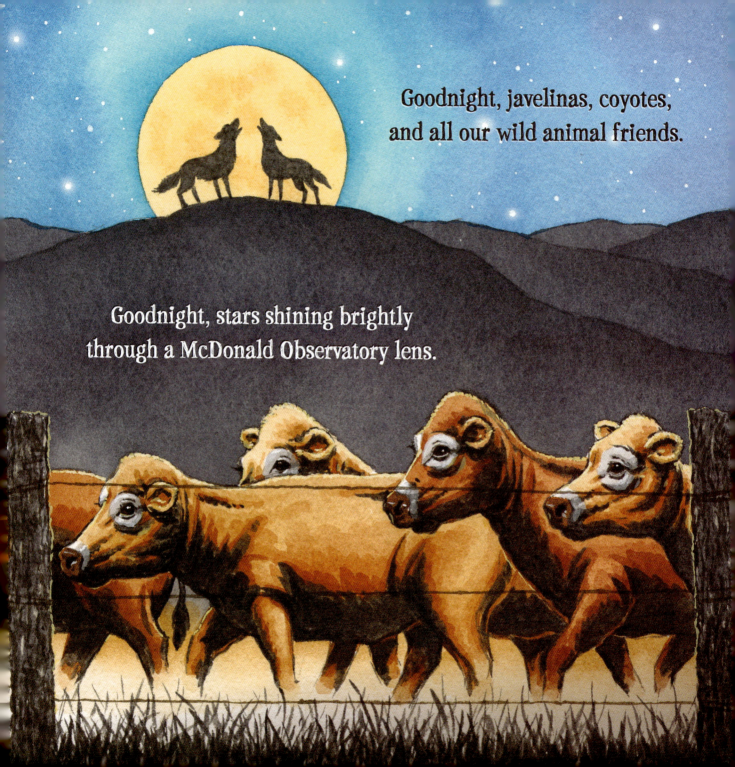

Goodnight, javelinas, coyotes,
and all our wild animal friends.

Goodnight, stars shining brightly
through a McDonald Observatory lens.

Goodnight, cattle grazing in the Fort Davis Mountains, so grand.

Goodnight to all the ranchers who care for our livestock and land.

Goodnight, Marfa artists and cowboys,
and everyone in between.

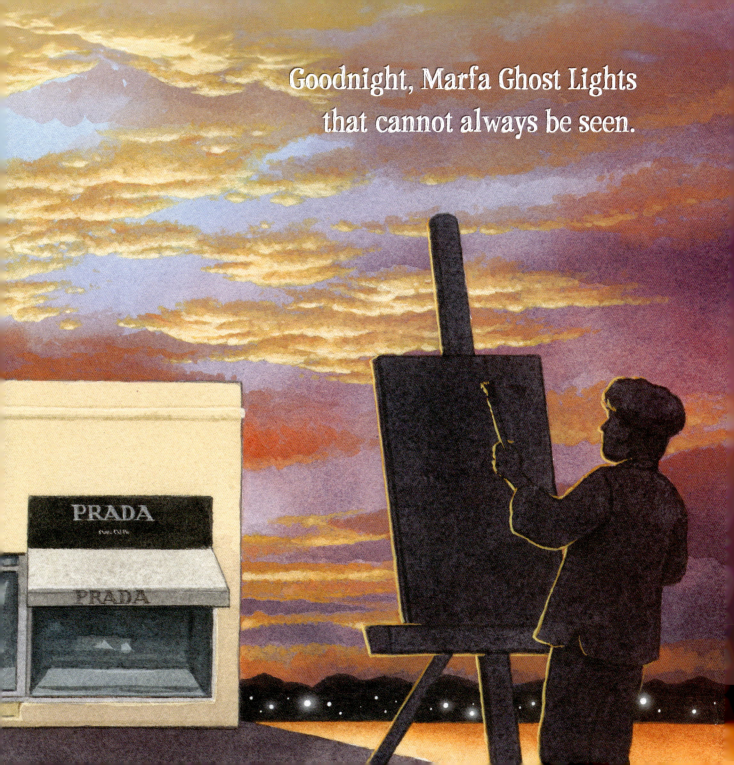

Goodnight, Marfa Ghost Lights
that cannot always be seen.

Goodnight, Alpine
and the baseball players
at Kokernot Field.

Goodnight to a town
where the true beauty of
the West is revealed.

Goodnight, Big Bend Saddlery. We love to shop and say, "Hello!"

BigBend

SADDLERY

Goodnight, leather work, saddles, and more. You're the "Best in Show!"

Goodnight, hikers and campers
out exploring Big Bend.

Goodnight, everyone enjoying
all West Texas has to lend.

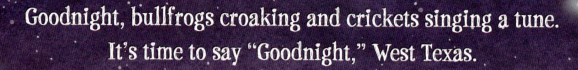

Goodnight, bullfrogs croaking and crickets singing a tune.
It's time to say "Goodnight," West Texas.

WE LOVE YOU!